OH! THOSE CRAZY DOGS!

TEDDI BEARS'
FIRST TIME AT THE LAKE

BOOK THREE

CAL

Illustrated by Rachael Plaquet

To order additional copies of this book, contact:
Xlibris
844-714-8691
www.Xlibris.com
Orders@Xlibris.com

ISBN: 978-1-6641-1140-0 (sc)
ISBN: 978-1-6641-1141-7 (hc)
ISBN: 978-1-6641-1139-4 (e)

Library of Congress Control Number: 2021921029

Print information available on the last page.

Rev. date: 10/11/2021

Introduction

This is a story about two crazy dogs, their adventures, and the mischief they get into.

They are very loving dogs, but they can't help getting into things.

Hi! I'm Colby! I'm big and red and furry! I love everyone but sometimes people are afraid of me because I am so big!

Hi! I'm Teddi Bear! I'm big and white and very furry! I'm not as big as Colby but just about. Everyone thinks I'm cute and I put on shows for them.

Our owners picked us out specially and brought us home to love and care for us. We love them too, very much. They give us everything and a warm loving home. We will call them Mom and Pop.

Sometimes we don't listen to them, especially me, Teddi Bear!

Our mom and pop love us anyway. Sometimes I get Colby in trouble. I can get him to do anything I want because he loves me too and can't say no. He protects me all the time.

Teddi Bear's First Time at the Lake

Mom and Pop were hurrying around at home, packing up food and clothes, pots and pans, and our food bowls and our blankets! Some of our toys too!

Their were taking all our food and bones and treats. "Hey, Colby, are they giving us away? What is going on? What is happening?" asked Teddi Bear and he ran and hid under a chair.

Colby laughed and said, "I think we are going to the cottage!
I love the cottage!"

"What is a cottage?" asked Teddi Bear.

"The cottage is a house at the lake, our house," replied Colby.

"We can run around all over the place, and Mom and Pop don't care!"

"Why don't they care?" asked Teddi Bear.

"Because it is a great big yard, and we can run around and play in the sand and the lake," replied Colby.

"We can swim, sometimes with Mom. She swims far and lets me chase her! It is so much fun! But we have to go for a very long van ride to get there, and you have to be a good dog or they won't take you. The van ride is boring, but we get lots of petting on the way there."

"Okay," said Teddi Bear, and he came out from under the chair.

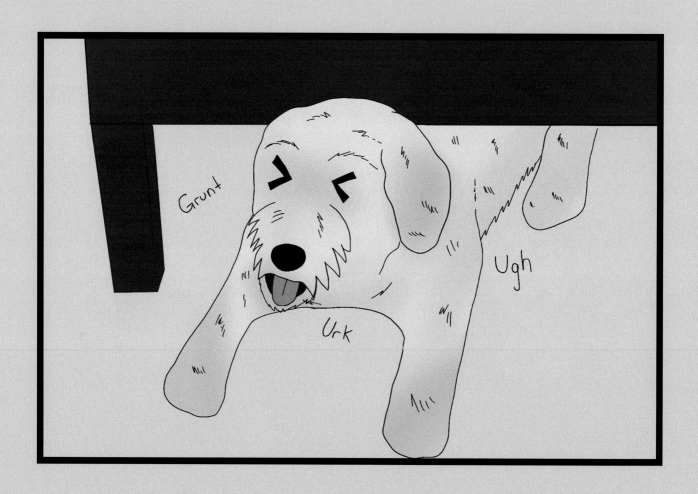

"Come on, boys, let's go for a ride," said Mom and Pop. And Teddi Bear followed Colby into the van.

Then they started out on their new journey.

Teddi Bear would bark at people who were walking across the street and when they were stopped at red lights in the towns they were passing through.

Colby lay down beside Mom and Pop in the front with his back legs tucked under the middle bench seat, and Teddi Bear sat in the middle seat looking out the window most of the way.

We stopped at a gas station, and when we were finished gassing up, we drove to a field so we could run around and play and go to the bathroom.

Then we got back into the van, and we drove to a takeout restaurant. We already had all our food and water on the floor in the van, but we still begged for their food. They always gave us a tiny taste of their food.

It was a long ride, but we were good dogs. One time Teddi Bear tried to jump onto Mom's lap while she was driving; that didn't go over too well. Pop grabbed him away pretty fast, and Mom yelled at him. He went back to looking out the window in the middle seat.

That was fun!

Finally, we got to a nice house and a great big yard with lots of trees.

As soon as Pop opened the van door, Colby took off really fast, and I followed him.

Down some stairs, across some pretty good-looking sand, and into the biggest pool I have ever seen!

Colby told me it is a lake, not a pool, and I was scared and put the brakes on.

My mom was laughing, and she kept telling me to go in. "Go swim with Colby!" she said. "I'll come in later after I have finished unpacking."

Colby kept telling me to come in with him. I put one foot in slowly and took it out quickly. I tried again and slowly put my other foot into the water.

Colby swam farther away, and I thought it looked okay, and Colby looked like he was having fun. So in I went too.

This lake wasn't calm like our pool. It had big waves, but I swam over them anyway. It was fun! You could swim forever.

Finally, we swam out of the lake, jumping waves, and I threw myself into the sand and rolled around and kicked up my feet. The sand was being kicked everywhere! This was so much fun!

Teddi was no longer white; he was full of sand. Colby was sitting with Mom on her beach bed, and Pop was sitting in his chair near the firepit.

Mom said, "Teddi Bear, Teddi Bear, stop digging here. Go over there and dig." And then Teddi Bear proceeded to dig a deeper hole for him to sit in.

I got up, covered in sand, and shook all over the place, covering my mom and pop and all the seats—everything. Mom and Pop yelled, "Hey!" and I started digging another great big hole.

My mom was just staring at me and said, "Oh no! We will never get all that sand out of his fur!"

Pop said, "Don't worry, I'll put him back in the lake and wash out as much sand as I can just before we go back up to the cottage."

Colby was just damp and not dirty. He was sitting with Mom on her big beach chair that looked like a bed. Colby was a good dog. He was allowed to sit on the other side with her because he stayed mostly clean, except his feet, but that was okay. Colby would sit quietly with Mom.

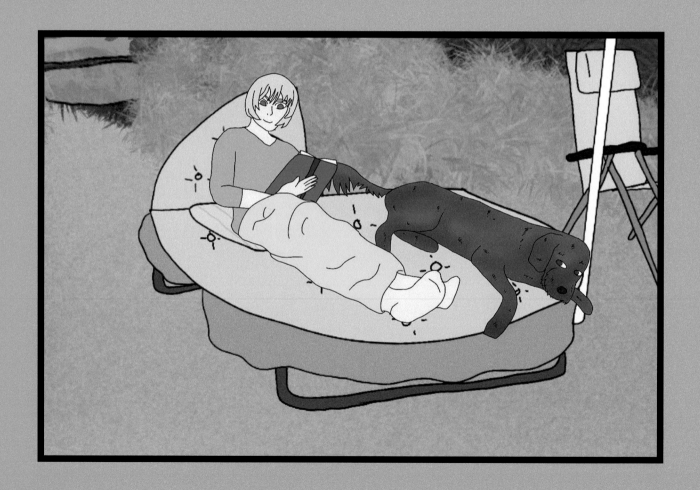

Teddi Bear went to jump on her big beach chair to join them. Mom yelled, and Colby jumped down, thinking he was in trouble.

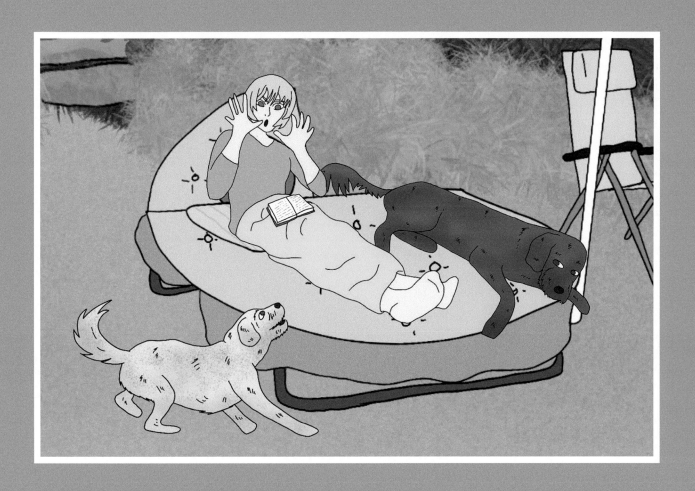

Mom said, "Teddi Bear, get off here. You are covered in sand! Go!" Teddi Bear jumped down, thinking, *I thought we were supposed to have fun! Colby was on the chair!* Too late, the beach chair was covered in wet sand. Then Teddi Bear shook all over and sprayed sand and water all over Mom.

Then Pop started throwing their balls into the water, and Colby and Teddi Bear raced to catch them and bring them back to Pop. Mom went into the lake to clean the sand off herself and to go for a nice swim.

We played like this for a long time. Then Mom got up and said, "We should all go up for dinner." Yay! Pop brought me into the lake and washed me off. He made sure I didn't have too much sand in my fur, and then we went up the stairs to the cottage. I raced everyone up the stairs and saw all the freshly cut grass. It smelled so good that I started rolling all over in it.

Mom saw me and said, "Oh no, he is all green now. What are we going to do with him?"

Mom told Pop that Teddi needed to be washed outside. She said to Pop that we had to stay on the porch until we were dry, so after Pop washed the green out of Teddi Bear, he rinsed the sand off Colby's feet. Then he put up a gate across the steps of the porch, and we lay down and watched the chipmunks run past us to eat the seed that Pop put out for them on the gazebo deck.

Boy, we wanted to chase them, but the gate was up. Oh well, we had a really good day, and we were tired, so we both had a nap.

I love the cottage too now. The next day, we ran around the big yard while Mom and Pop walked around it, checking out the flowers, shrubs, and trees she had planted.

We had fun out in the yard. Then we ran down the stairs to the beach and lake again and swam and played and chased the toys that Pop threw.

Mom went into the lake, and Colby swam after her and tried to get her back to the beach because he thought she went too far. Colby kept circling her to make her go back, but Mom kept laughing and swimming.

Teddi Bear asked Pop, "Why does Mom swim out so far?"

Pop looked down at Teddi Bear and said, "Your mom is a real good swimmer. That is her most favorite thing to do, and she's very good at it. She could probably swim right across this lake if she had to."

"Wow," said Teddi Bear. "Why does Colby stay with her?"

"Colby has a very protective nature, and he won't leave your mom until she comes back," replied Pop. Colby stayed with Mom until she came back to shore.

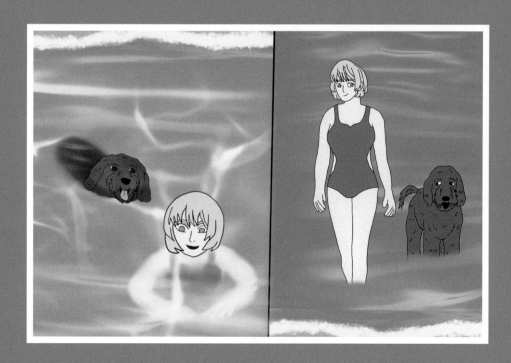

After a while, everyone sat in the beach chairs to relax, except me. I rolled in the sand again, kicking my feet in the air.

Then because I was hot, I dug a really deep hole in the sand and lay in it. It was cooler in the hole.

This is what we did every day. It was so much fun and different from what we did at home. Then I noticed Mom and Pop packing up and cleaning the cottage and putting all our stuff back in the van.

Colby looked at me and said, "I guess we're going home now." We were sad, but we could still have fun at home. We did the long van ride again; Teddi Bear looked out the window, and Colby lay on the floor between Mom and Pop.

When we got home, they let us into the house and then into the backyard. We ran as fast as we could.

And we jumped right into the pool.

Mom and Pop looked at each other and said,

"Oh, those crazy dogs!"

Thank you for choosing this book about the crazy dogs at the lake. We hope you look forward to the next book in this series where the dogs meet Digger and go on an adventure!

Oh! Those Crazy Dogs!

Series Written by CAL

Printed in the United States
by Baker & Taylor Publisher Services